# The Babe & The Librarian

## By

## Elizabeth Castle

Name: Castle, Elizabeth, author

Title: The Babe & The Librarian

Publisher: In The Air Publishing

Identifiers: ISBN 9781967731060 (ebook) | ISBN 9781967731077 (paperback) | ISBN 9798305488067 (amazon hardcover)

Cover Designer: betibup33

Chapter One

"Excuse me, Miss?"

Jenna "Mac" Mackenzie had to stifle her annoyance. One day she'd learn to take a flight home instead of the cruise ship. Too bad she was terrified of flying. But right now, she was tired and hungry, and the passengers who had just boarded were not her problem.

She turned to the man, intending to tell him no, but then did a second take. The man was tall and lanky, though his shoulders looked broad enough under the oversized Hawaiian shirt he was wearing. His legs were long and lean, like those of a runner. She had a nice view of them under his board shorts. He had a handsome, chiseled face, but what threw her was the oversized glasses that he had to keep pushing up his nose from the sweat that was gathering under the plastic frames. He looked like a man trying to fit the part of a vacationer but didn't quite pull it off. He reminded her of a college professor. Or maybe a high school English teacher. A sexy one.

"Yes?" She looked up into his deep brown eyes. A woman could drown in their deep depths; they were so dark, despite the glare on the clear lenses from the bright sun overhead.

"I don't suppose you work here?"

Her mouth twisted in a wry smile. She was a sucker every time. And she supposed she did work here. "I do. Can I help you?"

The tall man took a step closer. "I was wondering if you could help me."

Jenna saw the man's pale skin turn a little green. Figures. He was seasick and they'd barely gotten underway. It wasn't often a man caught her attention, so she continued to let her eyes wander. She was on vacation, after all, and he was cute. But she had no use for men without sea legs. Too bad.

She gestured toward the stern. "I'll get you fixed up. First time on a ship?"

The man followed her as her long, tanned legs ate up the distance between there and sick bay. "That obvious?"

Jenna climbed the stairs to the upper deck. "Sorry, but yes."

She opened the door to sick bay and pulled the tissue paper over the exam chair. "Have a seat."

The man sank into the chair, his pallor still green. "What's the prescription? Antihistamines?"

She glanced over at him as she pulled a box out of the cabinet without looking at it. "Did you throw up?"

He shook his head and turned a darker shade. "Not yet."

Since he wasn't complaining, she let herself feel a little sympathy. "I don't like drugs, unless they're all that helps. We'll fix you up with the wristbands. If they don't work, I'll give you pills to take with you to try. You can get more at the gift shop."

The man took the box from her so he could read it.

"Acupressure, huh?"

She could tell he was skeptical. "It helps some people. Not everyone. But it's better than a pill that will make you tired. You're on a cruise ship with the most beautiful view in the world. You don't want to sleep through it."

The man handed her back the box and looked her in the eyes. "It is a beautiful view."

Jenna stared at him. He looked to be memorizing her face. It was a cheesy line, but the look that accompanied it made her heart beat a little faster.

She cleared her throat. "Right. Thanks. You wear them like this so that the pressure is on the inside."

He watched as she took them out and adjusted them. "They're pink."

She huffed a little. "Not manly enough to wear pink?"

The man laughed, which was not the reaction she was expecting. "I guess I'm going to find out."

Jenna took a step back. "Seasickness may or may not pass. I'll get you a couple of packs of the pills in case the wristbands don't help."

He stayed where he was sitting, his eyes on her.

She pulled a couple of packs out and handed them to him. "Here you go. Instructions on the back, but hopefully it won't come to that."

The man tucked them into his pocket. "Thank you, Miss—"

"Jenna." She gave him her real name instead of the nickname everyone else called her.

"I appreciate it, Jenna. I'm Sean Cameron."

Oh, boy. Jenna knew that name. That was the name of the client who had hired her to take him out into the Florida waters to search for some old sunken ship. She had hitched a ride on the cruise ship to beat her client back to the office. She'd been visiting her grandparents and was on her way home. She hoped he found his sea legs. Otherwise, he might cancel on her. Though given her reaction to him, that might not be a bad thing. She didn't consort with clients. She didn't really consort at all. She simply didn't have the time. But he made her think of moonlight kisses and walks on the beach.

She took a step back when Sean slid off the chair. "You might also want to get a little something in your stomach if you haven't eaten. Nothing heavy. And if you do throw up, stay in your cabin. The cool air will help."

He followed her outside, back into the bright sunshine. "Can you point me in the direction of the restaurant?"

Jenna found herself leading the way. "Come on. It can take a little while to get your bearings."

He walked beside her this time, instead of behind. "What do I owe you for the bands and the pills?"

He did look a bit silly in the hot pink bands. She hadn't looked at the color when she'd pulled them out. "On the house, since it's your first cruise. And the ship's maiden voyage, at that."

He mumbled a thank you as they entered the covered restaurant. It was open-air, but the shade would get him out of the sun.

"Hi, Paul. Two cups of potato soup and a couple of baguettes for my friend and me."

"Sure thing, Mac."

"You don't have to watch over me." Sean followed Jenna as she led him to a small table.

Jenna caught his annoyed tone. "What? Don't want to share lunch with me?"

He dropped into a chair. "I'd think you wouldn't want to share lunch with me. I assume you're on the clock."

Jenna flipped her long golden braid over her shoulder. "I'm not working during this voyage, though I do work for the cruise company. I'm on my way home."

Paul dropped off the two cups of soup and bread. "Anything else?"

Jenna thanked him. "We're good. Thanks."

Sean eyed the cup of soup. "Cream can't be good for a sour stomach."

Jenna spooned up a bite. "Perhaps not. But the potatoes are. And the bread. Other than crackers, I'm not sure what else might be in the kitchen."

Sean fished out a bite of potato. He ate it. Waited. Then took another. "This is good."

Jenna tore off a chunk of the bread and soaked it in her

soup. "So, what brings you on a cruise ship?"

Sean mirrored her and tried the bread. "My parents. It's their fortieth wedding anniversary. Mom wanted to go on a cruise. Dad grumbled but gave in. It's easier to let Mom have her way. Mom saw this ship in an ad and thought it was perfect. It's a small ship and it doesn't sail too far out into the ocean."

"And you came with them?"

He nodded as he ate another piece of bread. "Mom insisted since I paid for it. Never mind that it cost more for me to come, but she wouldn't take no for an answer."

Jenna found she liked the timbre of his voice. He had a bit of an East Coast accent, but it wasn't prominent. She guessed he lived there but wasn't born there. "You're not sharing a room with them, are you?"

Sean made a face. "Gross. No."

Jenna giggled. "Good."

Sean leaned back in his seat. "I feel better. Thank you, Jenna."

She leaned back in her seat. "You're welcome."

Chapter Two

Sean watched Jenna as she walked away from him. The woman was something to behold. Her hips swayed as she walked, and he watched her until she was out of sight.

His son would call her a babe. And boy, was she. He'd seen her while boarding talking to some of the staff, so he had assumed she was working. She had on white shorts that showed off an incredibly long length of tanned leg. The button-up sleeveless blouse, also in white, had been pressed against her ample chest in the breeze. He'd been unable to look away.

She was tall. He liked that in a woman. He was six-two, and she had to be five-nine in her deck shoes. Those legs of hers went on for miles. Her golden hair was in a fancy braid and hung down her back, almost to her waist. He imagined unwrapping that hair against his pillow.

Her face, bare of makeup, was stunning. She had long blonde lashes, which told him her hair color was natural and not from a bottle. She had slightly tilted eyes the same shade of blue-green as the water that surrounded the ship. She had high cheekbones and the most luscious mouth he'd seen in a long time.

He wiped the sweat from his brow and took off his glasses that were sliding off his nose. Without them, he couldn't see much. His mother told him they made him look scholarly. His ex-wife told him they made him look like a dork. Both women were biased, though for different reasons. His mother adored him; his ex-wife barely tolerated him.

He wasn't sure what Jenna thought of him. At first, she looked annoyed. Then her face softened, and she fixed him up with the bands and the pills. He wasn't sure why she'd joined him for lunch. A woman who looked like that would have men tripping over themselves to talk to her. He'd barely said a word to her, other than to drop the dumbest pick-up line ever, and then tell her he didn't need a babysitter. Sometimes he was the dork his ex called him.

The man Jenna called Paul came to clear the table. "How was it?"

Sean pulled out his wallet. "It was great."

The man waved away the card Sean held out. "It's on Mac's tab."

Sean caught what Paul called her. "Mac? She said her name was Jenna."

Paul gave him a sideways look. "No one calls her that. At least, no one I know. She's always been just Mac. A few people call her Captain."

"Captain?"

"Yeah. I don't think there is a boat or ship out there that Mac can't handle."

Sean tucked his card back into his wallet as Paul took their dishes. Captain? Jeez. He'd asked the ship's captain, or at least the sometimes ship's captain, to help him with his seasickness.

Sean sank in his seat, a bit embarrassed. She hadn't said a word.

"Hey, son." His dad, Larry, took a seat across from him.

His mother, Carol, kissed his cheek. "Did you eat already?"

Sean watched his parents as they held hands and pored over their shared menu. Watching them, that's all he'd ever wanted. He wanted a woman he could hold hands with, pore over menus with, sit quietly with. Or not so quietly, in the case of his mother. He wanted to go to bed each night and wake up to the same woman for the rest of his life. He envied their relationship.

Sean cleared his throat. "I had some soup. I wasn't feeling well."

His father pointed to his wrists. "A new fashion statement?"

Sean gazed at the bright pink bands. "I was feeling seasick. A woman on staff hooked me up. They seem to be helping."

Larry shook his head at his son. "Only you would get

seasick in calm waters."

Carol admonished him. "Leave him alone. He's always had a delicate stomach."

Sean knew his dad loved him but didn't understand him. Larry was loud and brash. He'd worked in a steel factory his whole life. Sean knew he thought of his son as weak, though he'd never said so out loud. His dad didn't understand his love of books. Didn't understand why he'd rather read than play sports. Or go see a Shakespearean play over a basketball game.

Sean just sighed and leaned back. His mom liked to baby him. He was her only child. When his son Dylan was born, he'd had to rein his mom in from babying him too much. His ex was too practical to fuss, so it had been up to Sean to be the loving and supportive parent, but he hadn't wanted to coddle him either. His ex, Clarice, balanced him out, pushing Dylan to be outgoing and social. Sean wasn't either of those things, so he was grateful to her for being able to teach Dylan to be those things. Dylan was an odd combination of the two of them. He loved books, sports, and was outgoing.

Later that night, alone in his cabin, his thoughts drifted to Jenna.  She didn't look like a Mac to him.  Something about the name niggled at the back of his brain.  He knew his brain would eventually tell him what that something was.  He'd rather think about her curvy backside, ample chest, and long legs.  He drifted off to sleep and dreamed of her.

Chapter Three

Jenna left the ship as soon as it docked.  It had only been a three-day cruise, but it had been a nice break.  She'd seen Sean around the ship.  It wasn't so big that she could avoid seeing him, but she had kept her distance.  More times than not, he'd been in a lounger, his ugly Hawaiian shirt keeping him from burning under the hot sun, the pink bands on his wrists, with a book in his hands.  A big, old-looking hardback book, not a popular paperback or e-reader.  Put him in a pair of corduroy pants and a button-up plaid shirt, and he could be the stereotypical teacher she thought he might be.

She'd soon get to find out.  He'd hired her for the whole month to take him out on the water.  She knew from his email that he was interested in looking for an old sunken ship somewhere off the southeast coast of Florida. Most tourists never thought about what might be buried at the bottom of the ocean. To be honest, she didn't give it much thought herself. She'd rather take families out fishing, or on an ocean excursion, than try to dig up the mysteries of the sea. The sea could be brutal. Storm waves had sunk more vessels than anyone could count. She accepted it as part and parcel of life on the water.

Jenna stepped into her office. It wasn't air-conditioned, but the breeze from the water managed to keep the room from being stifling. In deference to the heat, she'd swapped her hot pink shorts and sleeveless blouse for a pair of cargo shorts and a fitted tank top with a built-in bra, so she didn't have to deal with layers. It was just too hot.

She checked her email and listened to her messages. There was a stack of paperwork to deal with, and bills to pay, but Jenna shied away from it. When Sean arrived, he had to give her half up front. Those funds would cover her outstanding bills. Her operation wasn't big; it was just her.

She supplemented her income by doing jobs like working on the cruise liners or taking out rich clients who needed someone to helm their ship while they partied.

Sean was the type of client she preferred. If he wanted to waste his time searching for a sunken ship, then she was happy to oblige. All she had to do was steer the boat. Maybe get in some fishing if she was lucky.

While she waited for him, she went and readied the boat. The cabin he would be using while he was here was ready for him. She'd had one of the women in town see to it that it was dusted, the linens refreshed, and the bathroom scrubbed. She hated housekeeping, but normally she would have done it herself. But she'd enjoyed visiting her grandparents and had opted to pay to have it done.

A booming voice from her driveway interrupted her thoughts. "Hey, Mac."

Jenna straightened as she finished stowing her fishing gear. Gavin was the local taxi driver. Jenna's property was in one of the ocean inlets and not a heavily populated area. She watched Sean's lean form step out of the back of the taxi.  Her heart beat a little faster at the sight of him.  He was still wearing an ugly Hawaiian shirt and board shorts.  He was also now sporting a fishing cap and boat shoes.

She jumped off the boat onto the dock.  She could tell the moment recognition hit.  He swung a large bag over his shoulder as he stared at her.  "Hey, Gavin.  Thanks for driving my client."

He saluted her after tugging an oversized suitcase from the trunk.  The man accepted the tip Sean handed him, and he took off.

Sean grabbed the pull handle of his suitcase.  "J. Mackenzie, I take it?"

Jenna couldn't tell what he was thinking.  "Yep.  But everyone just calls me Mac."

Sean had no choice but to follow her as she turned her back on him and headed into her office.  She took a seat and gestured for him to do the same.

Sean dropped his things and took off his hat as he gazed around the small space.  Jenna knew it wasn't impressive, but it did the job.  She didn't see the point in dumping money into the old shack.

Jenna shifted uncomfortably in her seat. "How is your seasickness?"

Sean turned his sharp gaze to her face. "I thought you worked for the cruise company."

Jenna leaned back in her seat. "I do. I also work for me. And whoever else is willing to pay me for my time."

Sean simply nodded. "You said in your emails you didn't have a problem helping me explore the area."

Jenna relaxed as they got down to business. "You're not the first treasure hunter I've met. As I explained, I don't have fancy equipment, but I've rented a submersible camera for you like you asked. The boat has sonar, so we're good there."

Sean pointed out the window. "That the boat?"

"That's her. It will hold a dozen people and will sleep as many. It's outfitted with everything you need. You tell me where, and I'll get you there."

Sean dug into his bag. He pulled out a handful of sea charts. "I've been studying the area, comparing it to my research.  These are the most likely areas where the ship would have gone down."

Jenna took them from him.  They were marked with tons of notes, with different areas circled.  "Can you read these?"

Sean took them back.  "I've been learning how."

"I can take you to all of those places.  Some will require overnight trips.  You didn't answer me.  How is your seasickness?"

Sean tapped his bag.  "Wristbands are in my bag.  They seem to do the trick."

Jenna turned to her computer.  "First things first.  I have contracts for you to sign.  Waivers that you understand the risks that come along with ocean voyages.  Then it's half up front, as we discussed.  Then I can take you to your cabin so you can settle in."

Sean read through all the papers she handed him.  Rarely did clients take the time to read the forms.  But Sean took his time, nodding now and again.  Seemingly satisfied, he held his hand out for a pen.  She watched as he boldly scribbled his name on the forms.

She accepted the forms and his credit card. She swiped it and handed it back and filed the forms. She grabbed her backpack from where she'd tossed it. "All right. Let's get you settled."

Sean looked around. "I don't see any cabins."

Jenna slipped on a pair of mirrored shades. "I keep thinking I should call them cabanas. But really, they're just small cabins that fishermen used to use. I modernized them when I bought the property. It's a short trek up that trail."

Sean kept up as he dragged his suitcase behind him. "You said there's internet, right?"

Jenna glanced back at him. "In this day and age, my business would go under if I didn't. Sometimes it goes out when there are storms, but we're not expecting any major storms soon. Anyone who spends any time around the water knows to watch the weather."

They were both sweating by the time she opened the door to the first of the two cabins. The interior was cool. Sean preceded her when she held the door for him. The cabin was bright and nicely decorated. She'd asked the designer to keep it bright and easy to clean. The white tile floors made sweeping and washing easy. The room was full of blues, greens, and tans. The rattan wallpaper added a little island touch.

Sean peeked into the bathroom. "This is nice. Sometimes pictures can be deceiving."

Jenna wasn't annoyed. "I try to live up to my reputation. There is a small kitchen, but you're welcome to come to the main house for meals. Just give me a heads-up if you're joining me, so I'll know to make enough for two."

Sean set his bag down near the small table that served as the kitchen table. "Any other guests?"

Jenna tucked her hands in her back pockets. "I'm not a hotel. Only clients who buy my services stay here, though many opt to stay in town or at a fancy resort and drive in. But no other clients. You've booked me for the month. You've paid the fee whether we go out on the water or not. Cabin is yours for the duration. My cell number is on the fridge in the kitchen if you need anything."

Sean turned to her. "Why didn't you say who you were

on the ship?"

Jenna didn't have a satisfactory answer. "Didn't seem appropriate at the time."

Sean's response was a slight hum. "I pictured you as a big, burly man."

Jenna got that a lot. "There's a reason I don't have my picture on my website. And a reason I don't use my first name. People seem to think being a man makes for a better guide. But I'm good at what I do. You're in good hands. But if you have a problem with my gender, say so now."

Sean looked her straight in the eyes. "I'll see you at dinner."

Jenna felt the knot in her stomach relax. "Good. I'll see you at six."

Chapter Four

Sean sat on the bench and waited for Jenna to finish preparations. He enjoyed watching her more than he probably should. The woman was efficient, and there was no doubt she knew what she was doing. She handled the gears, the ropes, the sails, and everything else as if it were second nature. No doubt for her, it was.

And he certainly didn't mind staring at the smooth length of her legs. Every time she bent over, he wanted to slide right behind her. He was no doubt one in a long line of men who had lusted after her, but she didn't give off any vibes that she might be interested in him. She was beautiful, athletic, competent, and no doubt independent. He was a bookworm who easily burned.

Jenna glanced his way. "Want to come up and join me? Kids usually get a kick out of learning how to steer the boat."

He groaned inwardly. Apparently, he reminded her of a kid. Great. But he was curious. He'd never been on any kind of boat before. The cruise ship had been his first foray. This was different. "I'd love to."

Jenna untied the boat and pushed off. Sean followed her. She started up the boat's powerful engines. He watched as she deftly maneuvered the boat. She explained the buttons and gauges he was looking at, but he could tell her focus was on getting them out of the inlet and into open waters. He let her be and noticed she had his sea charts on a nearby table with plexiglass on top. She'd made some of her own markings on the plastic.

Jenna saw where he was looking. "We're heading to the closest location first. It will take around two hours. It's a wide area. I also think it's the least likely, given the notes you've got scribbled. We'll see if your wristbands hold up in a sailboat. The camera is at the bow. You'll want to read through the instructions."

Sean would, but for now he was enjoying watching his guide.  He could see the muscles in Jenna's arms as she guided them further out into open waters.  She continued in a loud voice, explaining what she was doing and more about the area they were headed.

Sean wasn't sure how long they'd been out on the water when Jenna cut the engine.  The blue waters reflected the sun overhead; the white sand shores looked like mirages in the distance.  The wind and salty air filled his lungs, and he felt his body truly relax for the first time in ages.  This wasn't the same as it had been on the cruise ship.  He felt like he and Jenna were the only ones around for miles.

Jenna left the helm, and he followed as she raised the sails.  She had him help her, showing him what to do.  This he liked much better.  No loud hum of the engines; nothing but the wind and the sails.

When they were done, he took a seat to enjoy the quiet and the breeze.  Jenna went below and came back with lunch. She also tossed him a bottle of sunscreen.

Jenna sat on the bench, their lunch between them. She was wearing nothing but a bikini top and shorts. Her entire body was toned. He couldn't think of any woman he'd been with that had defined ab muscles like hers. She wasn't built like a bodybuilder, but her body was lean and muscular. Her skin was golden in the sun, her long braid down her back.

He slathered on the sunscreen she'd tossed to him before they ate. Lunch was fruit and sandwiches. He found himself ravenous.

She leaned back after she finished her meal. "Want me to slather up your back?"

Sean glanced at her. Did he want her slim hands sliding over his skin? Yes. Did he want to expose his pasty white chest to this beautiful woman? Not so much. He thought he looked good. He worked out and kept fit. He also loved to run. But no doubt he didn't measure up to the tanned, athletic men he'd seen around the docks.

Jenna grabbed the bottle. "Come on. It's too hot out here to have that shirt on."

Sean looked down at his shirt.  It was sticking to the sweat on his skin.  He'd bought it and others just like it, thinking they'd be breezy, but he'd been wrong.  Instead of second-guessing himself, he yanked the shirt off over his head.

Jenna came up behind him.  He jumped at the touch of her hands.  "We'll be near the location on your chart soon. Keep the hat on.  Next time we'll need to see about some sunglasses.  We can order some for you when we get back tonight."

Sean had to keep himself from stretching like a cat under her hands.  She smeared the cream over his entire back, shoulders, neck, and even his ears.  He could have wept when she was finished.  He stayed in his seat as she handed him the bottle.  He didn't want her to see the very physical reaction his body had to her touch.  Gritting his teeth, he slathered his chest.

Once his body was under control, he went to the camera she'd rented for him.  He was here for a reason, though he was struggling to remember that in Jenna's presence.

"I don't know how to work those. I assume you swim, though."

Sean shook his head. "Actually, no."

Jenna's eyes were wide in shock. "You don't swim?"

Sean got defensive. "Is that a crime?"

Jenna stepped back. "No."

Sean set the instructions aside. "Sorry. I didn't mean to be abrupt. No, I don't swim. This whole trip is out of my comfort zone in so many ways."

Jenna gazed up at the sky, adjusted the sails, and turned back to him. "What do you do for a living?"

Sean didn't want to answer her. He really didn't. He hated the way women looked at him. Or the way men would make fun of him. He liked his work. In fact, he loved it. But it was hard to make people outside academia understand that.

Jenna didn't ask again when he didn't answer her. She instead picked up their meal and went below deck.

Sean was looking at his hands when she came back. "I'm a librarian."

Jenna's mouth went slack for a moment. He knew what came next. Jokes about old ladies in orthopedic shoes. Or making shushing noises and exclaiming they'd better be quiet, or he'd get mad and toss them out.

Jenna did the opposite. "Don't you have to have a master's degree for that?"

Sean's head jerked up. Her face wasn't mocking him. She wasn't looking at him like he had two heads. She looked, well, curious. "You do."

Jenna tossed him a bottle of water. "I've never met a librarian before, and I meet lots of people. The only librarian I remember is when I was in grade school. She was the sweetest lady. She would ask you what you liked, and she would find the perfect book for you. I'd forgotten about her. I thought you were a teacher or something. I wasn't too far off the mark, I guess."

Nerd, dork, bookworm. He'd been called them all over the years. In college, he'd been nicknamed Einstein. He had toyed with studying education, but years of being called names and being made fun of for being smart and liking to read made him withdraw. The idea of teaching the same name-calling kids or adults never appealed.

Jenna sat back down. "Where do you work?"

Sean chugged his water. "Nowhere right now. I quit my job. I've been doing freelance research. Keeps me busy."

"Researching what? Sunken ships?"

Sean relaxed. "That was for me, but I research all sorts of things. My last job, I did research for an author who wanted to know more about the jungles in South America: plants, animals, survival, and their economy."

Jenna smiled at him. "You sound like you love it. What made you interested in a sunken ship? Treasure hunters often spend years, if not decades, trying to find that elusive treasure."

Sean didn't correct her. He wasn't looking for sunken treasure. As far as he could tell, the ship had been full of textiles. He didn't know how to explain to her his sudden need for an adventure. His son had started college, and he'd felt like an old man. He'd been cooped up inside different libraries, including his own, and woke up one day and realized life was passing him by. He was going to be forty his next birthday. He had a nineteen-year-old son, an ex-wife, and his job. And that was all he had. One day it had been enough. The next, it hadn't. He had been doing research on ships when he'd stumbled upon some references of an old ship that had sunk in the Atlantic somewhere near Florida. He'd become obsessed with finding it, taking the time to go on an adventure.

He doubted Jenna would understand that. Her entire life was an adventure. She sailed the ocean. She owned her own business. She was friendly, outgoing, and helpful. She'd helped a stranger struggling with seasickness and fed him a meal. And she was stunning.

Instead of continuing the conversation, he went back to reading the instruction manual on how to use the camera.

Chapter Five


"I feel like an idiot."

Jenna cinched the life jacket tighter across Sean's chest. It was a nice chest, too. He could use more sun, but she'd been surprised to find he had some nice muscle definition under his clothes. She thought he'd be skinny under the ugly shirts he wore, but she'd been pleasantly surprised. He was a client, so she certainly wasn't going to comment on it, but he wasn't hard on the eyes. Not at all.

She liked him. She liked spending time with him. He'd only been here a week, but she'd gotten used to having him around. He was smart and had a dry sense of humor. He was quiet and sometimes seemed a little shy. Definitely introspective. Most men she knew were macho, always trying to show off. Or heaven help her, the ones who wanted to prove they were better than her. They were the big strong man, and she was the little woman. But Sean wasn't like that. He asked questions about what she was doing and why. He listened like he truly wanted to know.

She wasn't ignorant of the heat she sometimes saw in his eyes. She'd catch him watching her while she worked. Some men made her feel uncomfortable. Sean looked at her with male appreciation in his eyes, but it didn't make her shy away from him. Which was why she was with him today, giving him his first swimming lesson.

"Hey, the jacket isn't pink. What more could you ask for?"

Sean grumbled. "I'm the only grown man around here in a life jacket."

She took his hand and led him to the end of the pier. "The water here is over your head. You're just going to relax and float and get used to it. Then we'll start with some basic arm paddling. Just think of this as research. If you fall off the boat, you need to be able to swim your way to safety."

Jenna stripped down to her bathing suit. She'd opted for a one piece for their lesson. She couldn't help but feel an answering heat when his gaze took in her suit. She felt his eyes linger on her cleavage a moment too long. "Eyes up here, Sean."

He turned beet red, but his eyes were hidden behind the clip-on shades on his glasses. "Sorry."

Jenna dove into the water. When she came up, she shook the water off her face. "Just sit on the edge and ease yourself down. You might feel a bit of panic when there is nothing under your feet, but the jacket will keep your head above water."

Sean did as he was instructed. He sank carefully into the water. "And why am I doing this again?"

"Because there is a storm to the south and we're staying close to shore today. And since you're already paying me, you might as well take advantage of my time and learn to swim."

Sean was tense in the water. "A very fiscally responsible

action on my part."

Jenna laughed and swam a little further out. "Exactly."

She demonstrated what she wanted him to do. He was so tense; it was surprising he could move. She swam back to him. "Sean, relax. I've been swimming my whole life. You like to run, don't you? Think of this as running in water."

Sean tried again. "How do you know I run?"

Jenna flipped onto her back and floated as he started to make headway towards her. "I know a runner's body when I see one."

"Yeah? This isn't so bad."

Jenna had him do laps around the pier. She saw him stifle laughter when fish were nibbling on his legs and feet. He was ticklish. Her heart did a little flip in her chest. It was safe to say that she really liked Sean.

She eventually brought him closer to the shore. There were people off in the distance, but he was no longer paying attention to them. Once they were back on solid footing, with the water about waist-high, she started unfastening his jacket. "Not bad, Sean. We'll eat, and then we can come back out if you want."

Jenna froze when Sean's fingers touched her cheek. She looked up at him.

He took off his clip-on shades. "I want."

Jenna's lips parted. He made no move. She thought he wanted to kiss her, but he didn't move a muscle. She started to pull away.

"I'm sorry, Jenna. I shouldn't have said that." Sean finished removing the life jacket.

Jenna took the jacket from him and tossed it on the beach. Knowing it was a bad idea, and knowing that things could get awkward between them, she took a step closer. She set her palms on his shoulders. She rose to her toes and pressed her lips to his.

Sean set one hand on her waist. He cupped her cheek with the other. The waves pushed his body closer to hers.

Jenna wasn't surprised Sean was a good kisser. Something about the way he seemed to study and analyze everything around him made her think he'd made a study of women over the years. His lips were mobile on hers, as if he were memorizing the shape and texture of her mouth. He didn't slobber on her, he didn't push her to open her mouth, and he didn't demand control. He let her control the kiss and followed her lead.

Jenna gently pulled away, keeping her hands on his shoulders to steady herself.

Sean released her cheek. "That was nice."

Jenna laughed and leaned her forehead against his chest. That was an understatement. She could have gone on kissing him for hours. But common sense and her own insecurities when it came to men had her pulling away and ending the kiss.

Sean was the one who spoke first. "We should eat. I'm starving."

Jenna turned and walked out of the water. Sean followed but slower. She knew he was taking a moment after their kiss. She'd felt his arousal. It was hard not to with the waves rhythmically pressing his body against hers.

Jenna gave him the time he needed and went about

setting up a picnic for them.  She handed him a towel when he took a seat.  She grabbed the bottle of sunscreen.  "Turn around."

Sean obeyed and was still as she dried his back and slathered him up.  She took a moment to apply her own.  She handed it back to him.  "Now me."

Jenna turned her back to him.  She almost moaned as his fingers rubbed the sunscreen into her back, his hands sliding under the straps of her bathing suit and his fingers brushing near the sides of her breasts.  Normally she stuck with spray so she could do it herself, but she had wondered what his hands would feel like on her skin.  Now she knew.  His hands were smooth; no callouses for her librarian, but his hands were strong and nimble as he massaged in the lotion.  She wanted to pull those arms around her, but she fisted her hands to keep them from putting those hands where she really wanted them.

They were quiet as they ate.  She popped up the umbrella she'd brought, and Sean staked it firmly into the sand.  Her belly full and her body humming, she lay down in the shade and enjoyed the breeze.

She woke to soft fingers stroking her arm.

"Time to wake up." Sean's breath was warm against her ear.

She opened her eyes. Sean was leaning over her. She blinked and sat up. "I can't believe I fell asleep."

The sun was still high in the sky, probably after three. She'd slept a couple of hours. Feeling embarrassed, she started packing up their stuff.

Sean helped. "I figure I'll do a little research tonight. And I want to make a phone call. How about we both go wash up, and we can meet around six. We can make dinner together. Or we could go out. I haven't spent a lot of time sightseeing."

Jenna thought about the kiss and the heat of his hands on her skin. Eating in public seemed like a wise idea. "I know a nice restaurant where we can get some great seafood."

They were silent as they made their way back to the house. Her house looked almost exactly like his cabin, except it had two bedrooms and a much larger kitchen. He left her at her door and went to his.  Jenna let out the breath she'd been holding and went in to take a shower.

Chapter Six

The kitchen table was full of papers, books, and his laptop. He worked better in chaos. Jenna had come by a couple of times with fresh towels and changed his sheets. But he made sure she left his work alone. She'd shrugged and went about setting the rest of the room to rights. His ex-wife hated it when she came into his office and found papers everywhere and books piled on the floor. Jenna simply cleaned around them.

He pulled his head out of his papers when his computer called. He'd messaged his son an hour ago to call him.

Dylan's face popped on the screen. "Hey, Dad. How is the beach?"

Sean relaxed in his chair. "It's good. My guide has taken

me out a few times. Your old man got his first swimming lesson today."

Dylan's eyes widened. "Are you the same man who told me that if man were meant to be in water, he'd have gills?"

Sean laughed. "You wanted to join the Navy and man a submarine. I was trying to discourage you."

Dylan laughed back. "Ah, yes, I think I was ten. We toured that submarine on my birthday. So who is she?"

Sean glanced at the cabin door. "She who?"

Dylan shook his head at his father. "Who is she? I can't picture any scenario where you volunteer to learn how to swim unless you're trying to impress a lady."

Sean leaned in. "Her name is Jenna, and she's my guide. She was appalled when I told her I couldn't swim. So she took it upon herself to teach me. In case I go overboard and need to swim to safety."

"Is she cute?"

Sean sighed and spoke without thinking. "The woman is a babe."

Dylan's brows rose at that. "Wow. I thought you told me

women weren't babes, that they were ladies, and to treat them as such."

Sean crossed his arms over his chest. "She is a lady. A lovely one. Unfortunately, the only reason she's hanging out with your old man is because I'm paying her."

Dylan shook his finger at him through the screen. "You're not old. You're occasionally a little stuffy and boring, but you're not old. Just lighten up. If she's a babe, I say show her what you're made of."

Sean wasn't sure exactly what it was he was made of, but he did know he didn't want love advice from his son. Dylan was the spitting image of him; another black mark against him as far as his ex-wife was concerned. Dylan was tall and lanky, but Dylan didn't mind. Said it made him perfect for basketball. And Dylan did have a way with the ladies. Sean just hoped he didn't settle on any one particular woman until after he graduated college.

They chatted for a while and caught up when a knock on the door interrupted them. "Come in."

Sean's eyes widened in appreciation as Jenna came inside

and closed the door. She was wearing some kind of jumper, except it had shorts instead of pants. The soft pink fabric molded her breasts, showcased the flair of her hips, and exposed those long legs of hers.

"Damn, Dad, she is a babe."

Sean glared at his son. "I'm going to kill you when I see you."

Dylan waved. "Hi. I'm Dylan."

Jenna came closer and leaned down so her head was near Sean's. "Hi. I'm Jenna. I didn't know your dad had a son. But I'd have known it just by looking at you."

Sean cleared his throat. "We're going to go get dinner. Behave yourself. And don't forget to call your mother. Save yourself a lecture."

Dylan groaned. "I will. The last lecture was enough to hold me through until next year. Love you, Dad. I'll see you when you get back."

"Love you, Dylan. Talk to you later."

Jenna took a step back. She tucked a small purse under her arm. "He's cute. How old?"

Sean closed the laptop. "Nineteen. He just finished his freshman year of college. He's on summer break, living it up with his buddies."

Jenna brushed back a lock of his hair. "Why didn't he come with you?"

Sean touched her cheek as she dropped her hand. "There is not a nineteen-year-old college student alive who wants to spend summer break with their parents."

She laughed. "No, I guess not. Ready?"

Sean checked his pants for his wallet. "Ready."

Jenna drove a jeep. She drove it as confidently as she drove her boat. That didn't surprise him at all. She seemed to be opposed to air conditioning. The nights he came over for dinner at her house, she had ceiling fans and open windows. Her office was the same. It was no surprise she preferred the open jeep. She pulled some sort of scarf over her hair as she drove, the ever-present braid coiled underneath.

Jenna pointed out different parts of town as she drove. She also waved at several people they passed along the way.

"Here we are. The best seafood place in town."

Sean eyed the building dubiously. It looked more like an abandoned shack. "The best, huh?"

Jenna looped his arm through hers. "Trust me."

There were tons of cars in the parking lot, so he let Jenna lead him inside. The inside was filled with tables and patrons obviously enjoying their meals. The hostess greeted Jenna by name.

"Hey, Mac. Been a while. Friend?"

Jenna pulled Sean along. "I know. I need grease. This is my friend, Sean. He's spending a month on the water with me."

The younger woman set the menus on the table. She jerked her head towards the bar. "Speaking of guys who would love to spend a month with you on the water, jerk alert at the bar."

Sean turned to see a large, black-haired man glaring at Jenna. The man made a rude gesture at her and turned back to his buddy. "Charming."

Jenna ignored the jerk at the bar. "Thanks for the heads-up."

Sean picked up his menu. "Should I be calling you Mac?"

Jenna rested her elbows on the table and dropped her chin into her hands. "If I wanted you to call me Mac, I'd have told you that was my name. I like the way you say my real name."

Sean wasn't sure if she was flirting with him or not. "So why Mac?"

Jenna kept her gaze on him. "When I was twelve, I decided Jenna was a stupid name. I wanted a cool name. If I was going to be a sea captain, then I needed something intimidating. Jenna didn't cut it. My grandpa always called me Mac, and I did and still do think the sun rises and sets on him, so I started telling everyone that Mac was my name. It stuck over the years. Plus, having a masculine-sounding name gives me more business. People are chauvinistic and think men are better guides than women."

"I don't."

Jenna grinned at him. "You're not like most of the men I know. Take that jerk at the bar. Rylan thinks that because he has a penis, women should kneel at his feet. You're not like that. Maybe because you're so smart."

Sean shifted uncomfortably in his seat. "Lots of people don't think being smart is a good thing. I can't tell you how many times I've been called a nerd or a bookworm. Or worse. And I don't mean kids growing up."

"I was intimidated by smart people, but I never called them names. You don't lord it over people the way some do. It's just part of you."

Sean didn't know what to say to that. Thankfully the waitress chose that moment to take their order.

Jenna sat straight up in her seat. "Do you trust me, Sean?"

The waitress nudged him. "Just say yes."

Sean relaxed. "Yes."

Jenna ordered their meal, as well as a couple of drinks. She then went back to her earlier position, chin in her hands. "So, you think I'm a babe?"

Sean almost spit out the water he was taking a drink of. There was a hint of mischief in her eyes. "I'm going to kill my son."

Her blue-green gaze didn't waver. "Then who will take care of you when you're old?  But you didn't answer my question."

Sean answered truthfully. "Yes, I do.  There isn't a man alive who wouldn't find you attractive.  You have a natural beauty, Jenna, and it's very appealing."

"That's sweet.  But beauty fades."

Sean set his glass down. "Not the kind that's inside you."

Jenna leaned back in her seat. "Wow.  Okay.  That might be the nicest compliment I've ever gotten from a man.  I'm not flattered when a guy tells me how hot I am, as if that's the most important thing."

Uncomfortable, Sean changed the subject, and they went back to chatting about casual things.  Jenna had asked him questions before about the ship he was looking for, but this was the first time she had asked pointed questions.

"What exactly is the ship you're looking for?  You've been vague on details.  But I've seen your maps.  We've been to three of the closest locations.  Sonar didn't pick anything up."

Sean dug into his subject. "I almost missed it. I was researching Royal Navy ships from the 1840s for a client. There was a ship called the Harwick. After I turned in my research, I was playing around the library, going through some old logs. Mostly handwritten journals that logged ship's contents. Anyway, there I came across a ship called the Harwick. I brushed past it, but then saw the date. It was built in 1819, long before the Royal Navy ship I'd spent time reading on."

Jenna thanked the waitress as she set down the plate and their drinks, and went about dividing the seafood platter between them. "What kind of ship?"

Sean accepted the plate and kept talking. "It was a sailboat with a steam engine. Traditional sailing ships were fitted with steam engines that used wheels, like riverboats, mounted to the sides of the ships. The old sailing ships were solely dependent on the wind and weather, but these ones could keep going despite unsatisfactory weather conditions. It was quite a moment in human history. Trade between countries soared."

Jenna dipped a tempura-wrapped shrimp into a sauce. "And cannons. Can't forget that the boats were often outfitted with weaponry. Piracy grew along with the technological advances."

Sean's enthusiasm grew. "I don't think that's what happened to the Harwick. The ship had set out from Britain in Liverpool, just like so many do today. This particular ship primarily carried cargo. I think a storm blew it off course and sank somewhere near Florida."

Jenna dipped the shrimp and held it to Sean. "Try this."

Sean took a bite, prepared to go back to his story, then stopped. "That is good."

Jenna popped the rest of it in her mouth. "You can eat and talk at the same time. I don't mind. Are you looking for sunken treasure?"

Sean dug into the food on his plate. "You can choose my dinner anytime. This is amazing."

Jenna smiled and took a sip of her drink. She nudged his glass. "And this?"

Sean took a sip and almost choked. "That's a lot of alcohol."

Jenna took a healthy swallow of hers. "Rum, specifically. My vice of choice."

Sean set it down. "It's good, but strong."

Jenna continued smiling as she watched him. "So, sunken treasure?"

Sean continued eating as he spoke, unsure which held his attention more, his story or his food. "Any treasure that might have been there would be gone. Tea and textiles mostly. Some spices and various manufactured goods. No gold or silver or gemstones, I'm afraid."

Jenna's shoulders visibly relaxed. "So more about its history, then?"

Sean set his fork down, his attention back on the ship. "If I find it, I'll turn it over. I'm not interested in disturbing it or its historical value. But as I kept researching it, I discovered it never made it to its final destination. It was supposed to land in Charleston, South Carolina. I think it drifted further south. I started studying weather patterns around the East Coast and currents mapped out in the early to mid-1800s."

Jenna stopped mid bite. "You could find all that?"

Sean picked up and waved his fork enthusiastically. "You can find most anything if you dig enough. I've been researching this ship for four years. I contacted libraries all over the east coast. I was even able to get access to an old maritime museum's records. So many old books are photographed, and the contents transferred to digital. It's an amazing time to be a researcher."

"Some of the next locations you have on your maps will be overnight trips. The storm to the south should be cleared by tonight. We can leave tomorrow morning. Like your steamship, I have engines, and we can leave whenever you'd like."

Sean stopped and stared at his plate. "I've got less than three weeks to find it. I don't know when I decided I needed to find the ship, but the more I researched, the more convinced I was that I could find it."

Jenna set her fork down and laid her fingers over his

wrist. "If anyone can find it, you can."

Sean stared at her fingers on his skin. He thought again of how capable those hands were. "That's what I've been telling myself, but my funds are limited, and I can't play adventurer for too long. Real life calls. I should start trying to find a new job. Freelance work has kept me busy, but it doesn't cover all the bills. Not when I've got college tuition to pay."

Jenna released him. "Three more years' worth."

Sean went back to his meal. He didn't want to think about leaving or for his time with Jenna to end. She didn't laugh at him for calling himself an adventurer. She believed he could find the Harwick. It was a nice feeling, but the reality was he wasn't likely to find it. At the end of the month, he'd go back to his boring life.

"Such a sad face, Sean."

Sean took a bite and slowly chewed it, thinking about his life. "I don't know how old you are, Jenna, but life flies by. I'm thirty-nine with a nineteen-year-old son, an ex-wife, no job, and an itch to find an old ship."

Sean dropped silent after that, concentrating on his food instead of what he couldn't have.

Chapter Seven

Jenna steered the boat further out into the water.  Sean was once again buried in his research.  She decided to head out to the furthest destination on his map.  If his theory about weather and currents was right, the ship was likely further from shore than closer to it.  She knew from some brief research that there were around five thousand wrecked ships along the Florida coastline.  She was going on the theory that most of the ones near the coast would have been found.  Though she knew that wasn't true, that most ships, even when found, were not always accessible in the depths of the ocean, she still figured the furthest spot out was the best one to hit next.

She found herself glancing at him from time to time. He was so focused, and she had a deep, feminine curiosity to find out if he could focus on a woman as much as he did those books. They'd finished their dinner last night, and when they'd gotten back to her home, he'd bid her goodnight and gone back to his cabin. There had been something sad in him, and it pained her to see it after the enthusiasm he'd had about the ship he was hoping to find.

She set the heading and went to sit by Sean. "How is it going?"

Sean pushed his glasses further up his nose. "Hot."

Jenna plucked the fabric of his shirt. "I keep telling you that the breeze is better on bare skin. Your son will be impressed with your tan by the time you leave."

Sean glanced down at his shirt. "I'm more apt to turn into a lobster."

Jenna laughed and reached under the bench to pull out a bottle of sunscreen. "Not on my watch. Take it off, and I'll slather you up."

Sean halted her hands when they went for his buttons.

"Jenna, don't."

She stopped.  His eyes were hard as they looked at her. Uncharacteristically hurt, she got up and went back to the wheel.  She kept her back to him and didn't hear him come up behind her.

"I'm sorry, Jenna.  I'm in a foul mood."

Jenna kept her eyes on the horizon.  "You're entitled to any mood you want.  It's your show and your dollar."

Sean put a hand on her shoulder.  "And worth every penny I've spent.  I've been unsettled lately.  I thought coming here and embarking on an adventure was exactly the kind of break I've been needing.  But when I think about going back home, going back to my old life, it feels stifling."

Jenna knew how he felt, though for a different reason. "Sean, you're only thirty-nine.  You make it sound like you're an old man. You've only got eight years on me. You don't have to go back to your old life.  You can use this opportunity as a way to find a different way forward."

Sean took a step back and dropped onto the nearby bench.  "I know being a librarian is not the job little boys dream of. They want to be sports stars or astronauts. I like being a librarian. I love the people, the kids, and the scents and textures of old books. I wasn't a fan of the bureaucracy, which is why I ultimately quit my job and focused on research. When I was a kid, I lived in the library. On Saturdays, I'd spend my whole day there. I wasn't out with other kids; I was living an adventure in a book. Or learning about things I couldn't have conceived of in my own mind. I don't know when I realized I missed out on seeing all the things I've read about. And then I came here, and I met you. There is so much beauty surrounding you; you live the life I've only read about."

Jenna hurt at the sadness in his words, another uncharacteristic feeling for her. "I think it's amazing what you've accomplished. I know you have a master's degree. You have a handsome son. So maybe you haven't seen all the places you've read about. You're seeing some of them now. Maybe life can't always be a grand adventure, but trust me, life out on the open sea can get lonely. There's a reason sailors wrote about sirens and mermaids."

Sean considered that. "You'd make a great mermaid."

Jenna took a seat next to him. "What does thirty-nine-year-old Sean want?"

Sean's hands fisted at his side. "There's a loaded question."

Jenna supposed it was. "Okay. I'm on that list. What else?"

Sean's mouth opened, but no words formed.

Jenna touched a finger to his lips. "You did say I was a babe. But lust is easy. And it's transient."

Sean turned to face her. "It's not transient, Jenna. It's pretty persistent. But to answer your real question, I want the feeling I had when I first graduated. The feeling that there was so much life to be had. I can admit I made a mistake marrying so young. I was wondering how to get myself out of it when Clarice said she was pregnant. We were barely nineteen. She dropped out of college, but I stayed, though it took me longer to earn my degree because I was working full time. I wasn't willing to give up my education, even though I loved Dylan the moment he was born.   Clarice didn't understand why I wasn't studying business, or law, or something that would make us wealthy."

Jenna brushed her fingers against his hairline. "It's not who you are."

Sean nodded.  "Clarice didn't understand that.  She eventually got her law degree.  She filed for divorce the day she passed her bar exam."

Jenna trailed her fingers down his cheek.  "You don't sound torn up about it."

Sean set a hand on her knee.  "I wasn't, and I'm not. Dylan was fourteen and just starting high school.  I don't think either of us missed her that much when she left.  She and Dylan are close, but the distance is probably why they are.  Clarice isn't one to pull punches or coddle, not even with her son."

Jenna shifted so that her knee was between his.  "She doesn't sound like the woman for you."

Sean pulled back. "Jenna?"

Jenna scooted closer and pressed her lips to the skin behind his ear. "Yes?"

"What are you doing?"

Jenna thought about it. "I've got this uncharacteristic urge to seduce you."

## Chapter Eight

Sean inhaled when she bit his ear. "Uncharacteristic?"

She nibbled his neck. "Yes, uncharacteristic. Like when you hurt my feelings when you pulled away from me. And when you made me feel sad because of the pain I could hear in your voice. I'm not usually driven by emotion. I'm a very practical woman; emotions get in the way."

Sean's hand tightened on her knee. "Am I supposed to protest or something?"

Jenna brought her mouth to his. "I hope not."

Sean's arms came around her, his knees spreading so he could pull her closer. "Don't you need to steer the boat or something?"

Jenna stood, took his hand, and pulled her with him.

"Technology is a wonderful thing. We're on course to reach our destination by night fall. We'll anchor and start charting out the area in the morning and do a grid search like we did last time. But we're a good two hours away."

Sean's eyes darkened as he followed her into the cabin. "I don't think this is going to take two hours."

Jenna laughed and slid her hand into his board shorts and found what she was looking for. "Maybe not. I'm thinking ten, maybe fifteen minutes."

Sean groaned as her fingers stroked him. "Keep that up, and it will be over now."

Jenna pulled him down on top of her onto the small bed. She wriggled so she could reach the ties of her bikini top.

Sean's hands stopped her. "Let me."

Jenna grabbed his shirt and started unbuttoning it instead. "Okay."

Sean helped her with the buttons, removed his shirt, and tossed it on the floor. Her hands stroked over the muscles of his chest. He might never have a deep tan, but the paleness of his skin had darkened over the past week. She ran her hands over his hair-roughened chest, over his shoulders, and down his arms.

Sean levered himself up and pulled the ties of her bikini top. The fabric fell away, revealing her full breasts. She sighed in pleasure as his fingers gently stroked and rubbed her breasts. He was careful not to grab at her like she was some sort of squeeze toy, as one woman had once accused him of. His touch was firm but gentle; no way would he hurt her. His mouth replaced his hands, and her legs climbed his hips.

Sean lifted his head so he could see her eyes. "You have no idea what you do to me, Jenna. How you make me feel."

Jenna gasped as his mouth gently tugged her nipple. Her hips moved against him of their own accord. "How do I make you feel, Sean?"

Sean moaned as her body pressed firmly against his erection. "Probably like those sailors did when they saw the beautiful mermaid. Except you chose to stay instead of swim away."

Jenna squirmed under him. "Definitely not going to

swim away. Or walk away. Or anything else."

Jenna pulled his mouth to hers. He realized he hadn't even kissed her. It had only been a day, but he missed the taste of her. This time, his tongue did ask for entrance, and she gave him what he sought.

As they kissed, Sean's hand found the opening of her shorts. He slid them down her legs, along with her bikini bottoms. He pulled his mouth from hers to finish removing her clothes, tracking his fingers across her belly. "No tan lines."

Jenna found that hilarious. "I'll show you how to achieve that. First you have to remove your shorts, too."

Sean got to his feet and stripped off the rest of his clothes. For a moment, they simply stared at each other, each taking in the sight of the other.

Jenna raised herself up to her elbows. "I had no idea librarians were so sexy."

Sean didn't laugh, though he was amused. "I already knew mermaids were."

Jenna sat up so she could pull him back to her. "This

mermaid wants you to hurry up."

Sean started to climb back over her, but then stopped. "I don't have a condom."

Jenna stilled. "I thought all men carried them."

Sean's hands clenched at his side. "I'm a thirty-nine-year-old librarian. I don't exactly have women throwing themselves at me."

Jenna got up, slid her arms around him, pressing her breasts and hips against him. "You have me throwing myself at you, so I guess I'll take care of it. Though, I really hope they're not expired."

Sean let Jenna go as he sat up. He stayed on the bed, his head hung, trying to catch his breath until she came back.

Jenna tossed one to him. "Not expired."

Sean looked at the box. "Just barely not."

Jenna shrugged. "You want to stop?"

Sean ripped the packet open and rolled it on. "It didn't tear rolling it on, so I'm going with no."

Jenna pushed him over and onto his back. She straddled his hips. She bent to press her lips to his. Sean kissed her, his tongue delving into her mouth.  He groaned and rolled until she was on her back.  He reveled in the feel of his body pressing hers into the bed.

Sean's fingers slid down past her belly, teasing her.  Her voice pleaded with him. "Sean, I'm ready when you are."

Sean groaned again, removed his hand, and spread her thighs wider.  Jenna gasped as he entered her body, filling and stretching her.  All he could manage was her name as she wrapped her legs around him.

When she lay limp under him, her body still pulsing around his, he held her to him as he whispered her name in her ear as he gave himself over to her.

Chapter Nine

Sean was relaxed as he monitored the sonar. Jenna was steering, but he saw her gazing back at him from time to time. After they'd made love, they'd dozed for a while. Then she got up, and when they reached their destination, she anchored for the night. She then pulled him back to bed, and they used another condom. This morning, she rubbed herself against him and stroked his aroused flesh. As she rolled the third condom onto him, she whispered in his ear, "not bad for a thirty-nine-year-old."

She made him feel like a randy teenager again. He had a hard time believing she was thirty-one, and when he'd said so, she'd shrugged and assured him she was as she pulled her clothes on. He was glad of it. When he'd first seen her naked breasts, high and firm, he'd started feeling like a dirty old man. But not so old that he wanted to stop.

The sonar blipped, and other than a school of fish here and there, there was nothing. He was so relaxed and so utterly satisfied that he could not have cared less about finding the ship. All he could think about was taking Jenna back to her bunk. Maybe in an hour or two.

Jenna came over and looked over his shoulder. She pointed over at the water over the ship's bow. "I was looking at your satellite photos. We'll head over there next."

Sean pulled Jenna onto his lap and nuzzled her ear. She tipped her head to give him better access. "I keep thinking how I'd rather take you back to bed than look for the ship."

Jenna pulled back and looked into his eyes. "You mean that."

Sean was confused. "Of course, I mean that."

Jenna brushed her lips against his. "Don't take this the wrong way, but you're nothing like the men I've known."

Sean nibbled on her bottom lip. "I take it that's a good thing?"

Jenna wrapped her arms around him, hugging him to her. "It's a very good thing."

Sean released her. "Good. Is it lunch time yet? I'm starving."

Jenna got to her feet and set about putting lunch together. "I notice you've stopped wearing your pink wristbands."

Sean glanced at his wrists. "Guess I found my sea legs."

Jenna gave him a sideways glance and tried to hide a smile.

"What?"

Jenna stood on her toes and planted a playful kiss on his lips. "I have no use for a man with no sea legs. Though I was going to make an exception for you, because you're really good at other stuff."

Sean pulled her hips against his. "Yeah, like what?"

Jenna gasped, rolled her hips against his, but then pulled away. "You know exactly what. But I'm starving too, so let's eat first."

He cleaned up after they ate as Jenna steered them

towards the area on the satellite photo she'd shown him.  He was relaxed, and at first didn't realize the sonar was making noise.  The sound got louder, and he sat up.  He had studied and researched sonar technology, but this was the first time he'd seen anything other than fish.

"Jenna!"  He shouted for her.

She shut off the engine and came over.  "Oh, my God."

Sean pulled her to him.  "The camera.  We need to get it in the water."

Jenna helped Sean.  The submersible camera was rigged to work similarly to any other remote-controlled device. The camera would capture live video and feed it back to the monitor.

Jenna left and came back with her scuba gear.  "I doubt I'll be able to see more than the camera, depending on how far down it is."

Sean was reluctant to let Jenna go into the water, but he knew how ridiculous that was.  She was a certified diver, among her many other talents.  He helped get both her and the camera into the water.  He'd been practicing with the controls, so he was confident he could use them.

For a time, he could see Jenna in the corner of the camera. He kept the camera in line with where the sonar was detecting a large object. The camera kept descending, and he lost all track of time. When the camera caught the first glimpse of the ship, a feeling he couldn't even begin to describe came over him. He'd done it! He, Sean Cameron, librarian, had found it!

He lost himself in the video footage. He barely registered Jenna climbing back aboard until her tank hit the deck.

She came, wetsuit dripping, and put her arms around him from behind. "It's amazing."

Sean nodded. The ship was in pieces, which came as no surprise. It looked like it had been laid to rest on a reef or an elevated section of the ocean floor. Funny, he didn't know the terminology for the topographical map of the ocean floor. Something he'd have to research.

He steered the camera, filming the entire area where he could see sections of the old ship. Wooden poles that once were the ship's masts lay broken across the deck of the ship. The largest section lay on its side, broken open where the camera could peer inside to what was once an amazing piece of human ingenuity.

He wasn't sure how long they sat there, but eventually, Jenna slipped the controls from his hands.

"The battery is going. We need to get it back on board."

Sean helped get the camera back on deck. He then saved the footage onto his laptop and saved another copy in the cloud. "I can't wait to examine the footage more closely."

Jenna pressed a kiss to the back of his neck. "Anyone ever tell you you're amazing?"

Sean stopped, realizing the magnitude of what he'd found. He turned dazed eyes to Jenna. "No. I can't believe I found it."

Jenna lightly kissed him. "I had no doubt you would."

Sean shook his head. "Wait until Dylan hears."

Jenna kept her back to him, leaving to stow away her gear.

Sean stood at the railing, his eyes focused on the surface

of the water, wishing he could see the wreckage with his own eyes.

Chapter Ten


Jenna changed the sheets on Sean's bed. She'd barely seen him all week. The first few days he'd gone over the footage, jotting down notes, pouring through printouts, and making phone calls. He'd grumbled that the closest library was four towns over. She assumed that's where he was today.

Jenna brushed back unexpected tears. He was just a client. Okay, so yeah, they'd had sex. Pretty amazing sex. She knew she was as guilty of stereotyping as the next person. While she had wondered if he'd have the same focus on a woman's body as he seemed to have on his research, she hadn't expected much. She'd thought he'd be, well, clinical was the best word she could come up with. No doubt he'd have better words for it. But he hadn't. He'd made a study of her from head to toe. Physically speaking, their relationship had surpassed all her previous encounters.

Emotionally speaking, she knew she was in just as deep. She wasn't sure what it was about him that drew her. She liked listening to him. Sometimes she had no idea what he was talking about, but it wasn't so much what he said as it was how he said it. Whatever had made him sad was now buried under a spark of enthusiasm. She loved her job; loved being out on the open waters, controlling her own destiny. But she didn't have the same enthusiasm as she'd had ten, even five years ago. Running her own business, putting in the hours of paperwork, had taken some of the fun out of her job.

She let out a frustrated breath and went to the bathroom. He'd be gone in a week and a half. She had new clients lined up. A family of seven wanted to get the full ocean fishing experience. Jenna couldn't fathom raising five kids, but she liked taking large families out on the water. The interactions between siblings were either amusing or annoying. The woman who had booked her had sounded excited, so she hoped they were amusing.

She pulled the towels off the rack. With the exception of the dining table, Sean was one of the neatest clients she ever had. Hating herself for it, she dropped down on the toilet and buried her face in his towels. She was going to miss him. Her heart ached at how much she would.

She heard his computer ringing, and she bundled up the towels to check. She saw his son's name. "Hi, Dylan."

The young man smiled at her. "Hi. Where's Dad?"

Jenna took a seat. "Not sure. I haven't seen him much. He was out the door before I was even awake. I think the last time I saw him was at breakfast yesterday."

Dylan chuckled. "That's Dad for you. When he's engrossed in a project, nothing and no one exists. I used to get mad about it, but it's just how he is."

Jenna tried to smile, but she knew she fell short. "This is a big discovery. Treasure hunters will be disappointed, but the historical societies will be ecstatic. He said one society wants to send out a proper dive team and start documenting it. Your father is in seventh heaven."

Dylan's smile evaporated. "Hey, he doesn't mean anything by it. When he finally surfaces, he'll be apologetic about it."

Jenna shifted the towels in her arms. "He's just a client, Dylan. It's fine."

He didn't look convinced. "I doubt he'll be back home anytime soon. He'll want to be part of the discovery team."

"It's the discovery of a lifetime. I'm happy for him. I shouldn't have been surprised that we found it so quickly." She didn't add how she wished she'd chosen the closer locations first. But she knew that was selfish.

"Just do what I do and be obnoxious until he pays attention."

Jenna found she could laugh at that. "I'll give it a shot. I'll tell him you called."

They said their goodbyes, and Jenna got to her feet. Somethings were simply not to be. She hoped he did take the time to join the team. He'd found his sea legs, after all.

Jenna was about to leave when she saw Sean's open

notebook. She'd seen him feverishly writing in it when she'd brought him his dinner last night. His neat, very legible handwriting made her smile. She couldn't even read her own. But as she read it, this wasn't research. She took the notebook with her. Once she had the towels and sheets in the wash, she took a seat at her small kitchen island. He was writing a book. It was about the Harwick, of course. She couldn't see him writing fiction. But his words captured her attention, drew her into the history of the ship, its various journeys, before sinking and sleeping at the bottom of the Atlantic. He made life on the boat sound almost romantic, luring the reader into the story he was weaving.

She realized she'd read the entire thing when she flipped the page and it was blank. The story wasn't over. Dylan was right. He wouldn't be going home anytime soon. But he would be leaving her to be a part of the story as it unfolded.

The sun was setting, and she went about fixing dinner. She'd lost hours of her day in his book. She was surprised when she heard a car door slam.  She walked to glance out the window.  Sean was making his way toward her door. When he knocked, her heart broke a little more.  He still acted like a guest instead of the lover from the other night.

She simply hollered for him to come in.  She kept stirring the pot of vegetable stew she was making for dinner.  Fresh bread from the local market was sitting on her counter.

Sean came into the kitchen, setting a new stack of books and papers on the counter. "Sorry I'm late.  I got caught up."

She glanced at the pile and her brows raised at that. "More research?"

He almost looked sheepish.  "I wanted to learn more about the other shipwrecks in this area.  It's fascinating to think there are over three million sunken ships around the world."

She grabbed his notebook where she'd left it and tossed it to him. "You've a way with words, Sean.  It's a gift."

He blinked as if coming out of a trance. "You read it?"

She glanced back at him. "I didn't think you'd mind."

He shook his head. "No. No, I don't mind. It's just that no one has ever read my books before. Except Dylan."

Jenna pasted a fake smile on her face. "Oh? How many books have you written?"

Sean took a seat in the spot she'd vacated. "This one makes ten. I told you; I get engrossed in my research. Most of the research I do is very specific. But I go down rabbit holes, and once I've turned over the requested research, I tend to keep going. I like to put all of it together. Writing books seemed like the logical thing."

She could smile at that. Trust Sean to write a book because it was the logical thing to do. She set a bowl in front of him. He ate automatically, his mind still on his research.

Jenna let him talk as she cleaned up. He barely said goodbye when he left. Hating the tears that stung her eyes, she cleaned up and went to bed.

Chapter Eleven

Sean rubbed his eyes, suddenly exhausted. He glanced at the clock. It was midnight. It had been a whirlwind since they got back from the ship. It would take time to get all the permits needed to do a full exploration of the site, but the people he'd been in contact with were already working on it. Sean would go home, finish up some other research projects, but then he'd be back. He had no intention of looking for another job when he could be part of the exploration team. He couldn't swim or dive, but he had a head full of knowledge and would help lead the expedition.

Expedition. He grinned like an idiot. He had hoped that he would find the ship. But not in his wildest dreams did he think it would still be intact. He'd spent time on the computer, snagging stills from the submersible camera. He'd printed out some of the better shots. He wanted to show Jenna, but he'd forgotten.

As if he were coming up for air, he realized he'd barely seen Jenna since their return. He'd spent every hour researching, making calls, meeting with a nautical archaeological society, and planning when he could come back. He had hopes that maybe Jenna would want to join them. He wasn't sure what the rest of her schedule looked like, but he wanted her to be there. She deserved as much credit as he did for finding it. She'd poured over the maps with him. Had gone through his notes and knew where the more likely locations would be.

He was sure that if it hadn't been for Jenna, he wouldn't have found it. He leaned back in his seat. He wasn't sure when it had happened, but he was in love with her. She was perfect. She was everything he'd ever wanted in a woman, but didn't think he'd have. She was funny, adventurous, smart, caring, and surprisingly sweet. He couldn't think of any other woman who would have taught him how to swim.

Who seemed to care and was interested in him, despite being nerdy and absorbed in his work.

He blinked, realizing that he hadn't spent any time with her since they'd made love on her boat. As soon as he'd gotten back, he'd dove into his research. He closed his eyes. Being with her had been the most amazing thing. More amazing than finding the ship, and he'd barely seen her or spoken with her since.

Calling himself every name he could think of, he yanked on his sandals, hopping on one foot when his toes got in the way. He grabbed his glasses and his phone. He used the light on the phone to make his way over. He took out the key she'd given him and unlocked the back door. He knew where her bedroom was, not that he'd been in it. If he hadn't been such a self-absorbed jerk, he knew he would have seen it by now.

When he opened her bedroom door, he didn't know what to say or do. It was midnight, so of course she was asleep. She was lying on her side, her arm tucked to her chest, her knees pulled up. Unsure now that he was standing there, he shut her bedroom door behind him.

He set his phone on the dresser, kicked off his sandals, and walked to the bed. He set a hand on her shoulder. "Jenna?"

She started at his voice, quickly coming up to her elbows. She relaxed when she saw him. "Sean. What's wrong? Do you need something?"

He set a hand on top of hers as he took a seat on the edge of the mattress. "Forgiveness."

She removed her hand from his as she lay back down. "Forgiveness for what?"

"For being a jerk."

Her eyes held his. "Okay. And?"

"And for being an ass."

She folded her arms across her chest. "Yes, that too."

He leaned over her. "I'm sorry, Jenna. Sometimes I forget everything else around me. When we got back, all I could think about was the dozens of things I needed to do. I got caught up."

Jenna turned back to her side, away from him. "It's fine,

Sean. I understand. This is important. The most important thing in your life."

Sean brushed her hair from her face, sifting the long, silky strands through his fingers as he realized he had never seen her hair loose before. His heart ached as he gazed down at her. "You're the most important thing, Jenna. I'm sorry."

Jenna rolled onto her back. He leaned over her, his arms caging her. When she didn't protest or push him away, his lips settled on hers. As his lips nipped and kissed hers, he groaned in the back of his throat. "I'm so sorry."

Jenna shifted and lifted the sheet in invitation. "Dylan says you do this a lot. Get absorbed in your research."

Sean stripped off his clothes and climbed into bed with her. He settled his body partially over hers. "I do. But there is no excuse. You're the most amazing woman, Jenna. And I haven't shown you that."

Jenna lifted so that he could get her nightgown off. He ran his hands up her rib cage to her breasts. She arched into him, as he reacquainted himself with her lush body. As he had done with her mouth, he nipped and kissed her all over her body. She sighed and returned the favor.

The room was filled with the sound of skin sliding over skin, soft words murmured in the heated moments between them.

Jenna shifted when he slid between her thighs. He grimaced when he realized he'd forgotten birth control again.

Jenna ran her hands over his back. "What?"

Sean pulled away. "No condom."

Jenna raised up and nipped his lip. "Again?"

He got up on his knees. "Again."

Jenna pointed to the dresser. "Top drawer. I bought some new ones. But you've been too busy to use them."

Sean went to the dresser and grabbed the box. "I'm a jerk and an ass. And a complete idiot."

Jenna held her arms out to him. "You're not a jerk or an ass. But I'd say you're an idiot for sure."

Sean rolled the condom on and settled once again between her thighs. He cupped her cheeks in his palms as he slowly eased into her body.  He brought his forehead to hers.  "Jenna, you're the most amazing woman.  I'd give up that ship in a heartbeat for you."

Jenna kissed him, urging him to move with a wriggle of her hips.  "Show me."

Sean showed her with his body what he didn't have the words for.  He loved words and language, but he couldn't articulate what she made him feel.  He focused all of his attention on her and showed her with touches, kisses, and his body how much he loved her.

Chapter Twelve

It was still dark when Jenna woke again. Sean was wrapped around her, his legs tangled with hers. He liked to cuddle, and she found that she liked it too.

Tonight had been different. He might not realize it, but she was all his. He pulled out emotions she wasn't used to feeling. He'd brought tears to her eyes with the way he touched her, held her, loved her. She didn't know how things would work out between them, but Jenna was determined to make this relationship work. She loved him. She wanted him. Smiling to herself, she vowed to make her librarian fall so in love with her that he'd never want to leave.

Scooching down, she settled under his arm. She was

completely relaxed and almost back asleep when bright lights were flashed in her face, and men shouted at her.

Sean woke, placing his body between hers and the threat.

"Isn't that sweet? We interrupted a tryst. Isn't that sweet, boys?"

Jenna held the sheet across her breasts, her heart pounding in her chest. "What do you want?"

The flashlight shut off, but there was enough light in the room to see the glint of metal from the gun the man was holding.

"We're going for a boat ride. Get up."

Sean's eyes were on the gun. "You don't need her. I can take you where you want to go."

The tallest of the three men came closer. "Can you now? I hear you're a sissy librarian. I'm guessing Mac here is the man in this relationship."

Sean's muscles bunched, but Jenna put her hand on his bicep. "Do what he says, Sean."

"Yeah, do what she says, Sean. Maybe you'll live to see the sunrise."

Jenna was shaking as they climbed out of the bed. Sean kept his body between her and the men as she pulled her nightgown over her head. She could feel the other men's eyes on her. She shivered.

The men were wearing Halloween masks, but Jenna knew who they were. She kept that to herself. Rylan was an ass and a lazy one at that. He'd been hitting on her since she grew boobs. He was an idiot if he thought she wouldn't recognize his voice.

"Let's get going. We don't have all day."

Jenna stumbled a bit, but Sean's strong grip kept her from falling. She couldn't stop the trembling of her limbs as they were forced at gunpoint to walk to her ship.

Rylan shoved her towards the helm while she watched the other two knock Sean down on the deck by the rails.

"All right, sweetheart. You're going to take us to the ship. It will be weeks before the permits are ready, and the crew starts the salvage. When they get there, there will be nothing left."

Jenna stared at him. "You think there's treasure down

there?"

"Why else would Loverboy have been looking for it? We heard him talking at the bar. Those old boats have coins, jewels, and all sorts of useless crap that people will pay big money for."

Jenna's hands trembled on the wheel as she waited. One of the men brought on board dive equipment. The other brought up a couple of coolers.

Sean was on his knees. "It's not that kind of ship. It carried textiles and spices. There is no big treasure to be found."

Rylan squatted down, the gun in Sean's face. "Bullshit. I've been waiting for a big score, and this one is mine."

One of the other men, Jenna was pretty sure it was Rylan's friend Deke, pulled up the anchor. "Let's get this show on the road."

Jenna glanced over at Sean, whose eyes were still on Rylan. "Leave him be. I'll take you where you want to go. But you're going to be disappointed."

Now that they knew the location of the ship, they were

able to get there by mid-afternoon. Thankfully they'd been given food and water. Rylan had laughed at her when she needed the bathroom, but thankfully he'd relented and let her go. She was grateful that he didn't seem interested in her. Any other time, she had no doubt he'd have used her to pass the time, but she could see his mind was on treasure. She shuddered to think what these men would do when they found out there wasn't one to be found.

The other man, who she was sure was his friend Jeff, just sat around drinking beer. She could tell the man was hammered, and she hoped that worked to her advantage. She had a gun she kept below deck. She kept it as a precaution. She did take strangers out on the water, after all. She'd never had to use it, but she knew how.

Rylan yanked her away from the wheel and threw her towards Sean. "We're here."

Deke started changing into his gear. "I'll go down and take a look."

Rylan waved the gun at him. "Make it fast. Just make sure the ship is there. We need to make sure it's here and get what we came for quickly."

Jenna wound herself around Sean, her eyes on Deke as he adjusted his gear and dropped overboard. He had a dive helmet and was able to talk via a mic.

"It's here. Must have landed on some old rocks or coral or some shit. It's not that far below."

Rylan handed the gun to Jeff. "Keep them still. I'll tie up the bitch."

Jeff's hand was surprisingly steady given how many beers she'd seen him consume. Instinctively she tried to fight Rylan when he tried to tie her hands behind her back. When Jeff walked over and pressed the barrel of the gun to Sean's temple, she quit fighting.

Rylan smacked her cheek, then pinched her chin. "Be a good girl, Mac. We'll play later."

Jeff took a step back. "What about the guy?"

Rylan dismissed him. "Pansy ass librarian. What's he going to do? Read at you?"

Jeff snickered.

Rylan geared up. "You two get nice and cozy. We'll be

back."

Jenna pressed her cheek into Sean's chest, and his arms wrapped around her. She was only wearing a nightgown, and she could feel the afternoon sun burning her skin. Sean, too.

Sean pressed his lips against her hair. "I wish I never found that ship."

Jenna turned her face up. "That ship is what brought you here. To me."

Sean hugged her closer. "This has been the best summer, Jenna. I had a grand adventure. I found a sunken ship. And most importantly, I found you. I know it's too soon, but I love you, Jenna. And if we get out of this, I'm going to prove it to you."

Jenna wished her hands were free. Ignoring Jeff, who was still holding a gun on them, she brought her lips to his. "I love you, too, Sean. You don't have to prove it."

The sound of Jeff opening another can of beer had Jenna hoping against hope that maybe they had a chance out of this.

## Chapter Thirteen

Sean helped Jenna get more comfortable as he glared at Jeff. "The least you can do is let us sit below deck. We're getting fried out here, and so are you."

Jeff's hand waved the gun back and forth as he continuously wiped the sweat from under his mask. "Rylan said you had to stay up here."

Sean glanced at Jenna. His voice was a whisper. "Rylan?"

She pressed her lips near his ear. "That jerk from the bar where we had dinner. I think that's Jeff. The other is Deke. I have a gun below deck, in the table next to the bed. There's also a knife in there."

Sean glanced up at the sun. He turned back to Jeff, his voice a plea. "Come on, what would it hurt? You've got to be sweating in that mask. It's cooler below deck. Your friends will probably be another half an hour at least."

Jenna piped up. "Longer. They had two tanks. They could be gone an hour. Come on, it's hot. You're hot."

The man finally tipped his head. "All right. You, pansy boy, grab my cooler."

Sean grabbed it, then helped Jenna off the deck. He quickly estimated the distance between him and Jeff. When they got to the stairs, he let Jenna go first. The man kept his distance, the gun on him. Hoping that the man was drunk enough, Sean trusted his instincts.

Sean gripped the cooler, and despite the tight space, threw it at Jeff. The man threw up his hands, dropping the gun as he tried to catch the cooler. Sean didn't wait. He slammed the door shut, locking them in. He ran to the table, grabbed the gun, and the knife.

The man was shouting outside the door, smashing it with his shoulder.

Jenna gave Sean her hands. She let out a groan as her arms relaxed. "Now what?"

Sean flipped the safety off on the gun. "Not sure."

Jenna laughed, but it was not a happy sound. "Rylan and Deke will be back soon. We need to subdue Jeff up there."

Sean jumped and Jenna screamed as bullets pierced the lock. Sean kept the gun trained on the door as Jeff kicked it in.

"Bastard. You think you're so damn smart."

Sean watched as Jenna picked up a heavy lamp. Sean's hand didn't waver.

Jeff saw the gun. "Yeah right, sissy, like you're gonna shoot me."

Jenna smashed the lamp against Jeff's head, and he went down. She was breathing heavily. "One down."

Sean looked around for something to tie him up.

Jenna ran to her dresser. "Satin underwear."

Sean smiled as Jenna used the knife to shred it. "What a waste."

Jenna glanced up at him, a question on her face.

"I didn't get to see you in those yet."

She grinned. "I've got more. I need to call in the Coast

Guard."

Sean followed Jenna back up. She radioed in their location and explained the situation.

Sean wasn't listening. He was keeping an eye out for the other two men to surface.

It was another twenty minutes before they heard one of the men. Sean kept them out of the man's line of vision, but he could see his face through the helmet. It was the other guy, not Rylan. He let the man get aboard and take his dive helmet off.

"Yo, Jeff."

Sean held the gun steady on the man. "Jeff is a little busy right now."

The man swore and saw the gun trained on him. Jenna had Jeff's. "Rylan is going to shoot your ass. Then we're going to take your girlfriend for a ride. Right, Mac?"

Jenna used another pair of underwear to tie his arms. She pointed to the doorway. "Go join your buddy."

The man cursed up a storm but went down the stairs. Jenna glanced at Sean. "I don't think there's anything down there they can use to untie themselves. Jeff looks like he's coming around."

Sean looked over the edge of the boat. "Keep an eye on them. You've got Rylan's gun. When Rylan comes aboard, I'll call for you."

Jenna bit her lip.

Sean glanced at her. "What?"

"Where did you learn to use a gun?"

Sean shook his head. "I researched them for an author once. Decided to go to a shooting range and try them out for myself."

Jenna came over and gave him a rough kiss. "I love that big brain of yours."

The sound of hands reaching for the ladder had them both turning. Jenna started edging toward the door, making sure Deke and Jeff were still tied up where she had left them.

"Not a damn thing. Stupid bastard. Who the hell searches for a ship with no damn loot?"

Sean held the gun on Rylan. "A librarian."

Rylan yanked off his dive helmet. The man's eyes darkened in anger. "Pansy ass."

Sean held the gun steady. "Pansy ass with a gun. Drop your gear."

It happened so fast, Sean didn't have time to think. As Rylan dropped his gear, he pulled what looked like a pistol out of a holster on his leg. Without a sound or second thought, he threw himself in front of Jenna as the man fired the weapon at her.

Jenna caught him as Sean sagged against her.

Chapter Fourteen

Jenna watched in horror as blood sprayed from Sean's back. She recognized the underwater pistol. She screamed as she caught him, the gun now out of reach when it fell from Sean's hand. She had also dropped hers when Sean's body landed on her.

"Pansy-ass librarian."

Sean got to his knees. "Leave her alone."

The man laughed. He yanked on Sean's arm, and Sean couldn't contain the howl of pain. The man kicked him in the gut. Then again.

Jenna tried to put herself between Rylan and Sean, but the man shoved Sean before she could move. She watched in horror as Sean went overboard.

Rylan pointed the gun at her. "Now it's just you and me, Mac. Beg me to spare your life."

Jenna knew she had only one choice. She threw herself at Rylan hard enough that he staggered back. Then she ran the short steps to the rail and dove off the boat where Sean had gone over.

She could hear Rylan shouting at her. One bullet zipped very close to her head, but she ignored it as she tried to see the surface. There! As she swam the short distance, another bullet hit the water, then another. The pistol he had held only four rounds. She prayed he didn't try to use the other two pistols on board or have extra bullets in his suit.

Taking a deep breath, she dove under the water. Thankfully, the sun was still shining overhead. She saw the blood first. She kicked harder and came around, her arms going around his chest and shoulders. She scissor kicked and was grateful Sean was limp in her arms. She cried in relief when he took a deep breath, then started coughing the second they hit the surface.

She saw Rylan at the edge of the boat.

"Let's see how long you and your boyfriend can tread water. Thanks for the boat, darlin'."

Jenna didn't waste her breath. She held onto Sean, crooning in his ear to hold still for her. She knew he was in a lot of pain. She wasn't sure where the bullet had hit him, but he was breathing, and for now that's all that mattered.

Sean took another deep breath. "I should have paid more attention during my swimming lessons."

Jenna wanted to kiss him but was afraid to shift her grip on him. "We'll resume your lessons when we get home."

Sean groaned and sagged more in her arms. She kept her grip on him, his dead weight now floating. She stared at the rise and fall of his chest, praying each time he took a breath that he'd take another.

Jenna wasn't sure how long she watched the rise and fall of his chest. When she saw a Coast Guard boat in the distance, she wept in relief. She waved, and it honked its horn in acknowledgment.

She waited as the men arrived. "I love you, Sean."

* * *

Sean woke in the hospital to an awful pain in his back. Jenna was sitting in a chair beside his bed, her hand holding his.

"Jenna." His voice was hoarse, and he winced. His throat hurt.

Her head popped up. "Sean. Thank God."

"What happened?" He touched her sunburned cheek.

"Do you remember being shot?"

Sean gasped as his body tensed. Curse words he never used came out of his mouth. "He shot me. He was going to shoot you. Are you hurt? Did he touch you?"

Jenna stood up, bringing his hand up between her breasts. "I'm fine. I jumped in the water after you. The Coast Guard saved us."

Sean was already tiring, but he squeezed her hand as she held it. "We got lucky. They made a mistake. They should have tied me up."

She pressed his hand to her lips. "He saw me as a bigger

threat. Big mistake. Never mess with a librarian."

It hurt to laugh, but Sean couldn't stop the bark of laughter. "The babe and the librarian. I should write a book."

She bent and kissed him. "Now you have a great ending to your book."

He cupped her cheek with the hand not attached to an IV. "Why does my throat hurt?"

"You're dehydrated. You sucked in some ocean water. Thank goodness your body coughed it up. I've never done CPR in the water before. And you look like a lobster."

He brought her mouth back to his. "I could have lost you."

She felt tears sting her eyes. "I could have lost you."

It was a long time before Jenna let him go.

## Chapter Fifteen

"Hey, Dylan, your dad is in his office again, with his nose buried in his research.  Go unstick his nose from whatever book it's in."

Dylan gave her a salute.

Jenna shook her head.  She had gotten the boat ready to go, and Sean had sworn he would only be half an hour, but that was an hour ago.

Her boat was no worse for the wear at the hands of Rylan and his friends.  The Coast Guard eventually caught up with him.  They hadn't had much choice but to surrender.  Jenna was just glad they hadn't tried to shoot their way out. All three were charged with kidnapping and grand theft boat.  Had they actually found treasure on that ship, there would have been a bunch more charges, but in the end, all they had done was investigate the ship; they hadn't found or dismantled anything.

However, Rylan was then charged with attempted murder. Jenna heard from the district attorney that he was going to cop a plea for a lesser sentence, but he'd spend a good long time in jail regardless. She was worried about when he got out, but she'd worry about that another day.

Ten minutes later, Sean climbed aboard, Dylan behind him. "Sorry, I got caught up."

She lifted her cheek when he bent to kiss it. "You're forgiven."

Dylan hauled up the anchor. "Wait until you find out what Dad is researching."

Jenna tipped her head like she was giving it some thought. "Another ship? No, probably not. I doubt it's sports. You couldn't even keep up with the basketball score when you were watching a game with Dylan. How about sea life? Or coral? You're becoming a much stronger swimmer; you were researching snorkeling. Or skydiving."

Sean set a finger over her mouth. "Did you know our little town doesn't have a library?"

Her eyes narrowed. "Yeah. You complain about it almost every day."

Dylan dropped down on the bench. "Dad much prefers books over computers."

Jenna bumped Sean's hip with hers and started the engine. "That's a fact."

Sean leaned over again and nibbled on her neck. "I prefer you over my books."

Jenna looped her arm around his neck. She shivered when he sucked lightly at her skin. "I noticed."

Dylan cleared his throat. "Dad, you're getting sidetracked."

Sean released her and sat beside his son. "Right. So I've been in touch with the mayor and the town council. They're giving me the green light to work on establishing a library. They're letting me use the old town hall building that's been empty since the new one was built. It's going to take some time, but I've already reached out to some of my librarian friends looking for some donations, or names of other folks who'd be willing to donate.  The council said that the building still had old tables, desks, bookshelves, and even some old computers.  They said I can have whatever I can use."

Jenna shut off the engine.  "You're opening a library here?"

Sean's eyes softened.  "I'm not going anywhere, and I am a librarian.  I need a library."

She came and sat on his lap.  "Can I help?"

Sean flipped her braid over her shoulder.  "You can make sure I don't get lost in my books."

She kissed him.  "Deal."

Dylan nudged his dad again.  "And what else were you researching, Dad?"

Sean pushed his hand in his son's face.  "You're a brat."

Dylan just laughed.

Jenna leaned back.  "Uh oh.  What is it?"

Sean took her left hand.  "Rings."

Jenna gaped.  "Rings?"

"Yeah. Rings."

Jenna thought about it, then wrapped her arms around his neck. "I love rings."

Sean murmured against her lips as she kissed him. "I love you."

Dylan got up. "Man, you two are mushy. I'll drive."

Jenna scooted so that her legs were draped over Sean's lap. The past month while they'd waited for the exploration of the ship to begin, she'd taught Sean to swim and Dylan to drive the boat. Dylan would be headed back to school in a week, but for now, she was enjoying having him around. "Just head straight out and head south for now. The crew is probably already there."

Dylan turned the engine back on and steered the boat slowly toward open waters. "Aye, aye, Captain."

Jenna shifted closer. "You know I'll say yes, right?"

Sean tightened his arms around her. "If you don't, I'll just research the best way to pick up babes."

Jenna laughed. Then she laughed harder. "I love you, Sean."

Sean cupped her cheeks.  "Best summer ever."

From The Author

Some of you may know it's rare I contemplate a novella. Some part of me is afraid that if I write a shorter story, the full-length novels will be harder to write. Now, it's not true. I wrote The Babe & The Librarian at the same time I wrote Chasing Hope, which is a full-length novel. But fears are funny things, and this book is only the second novella I've written.

The idea came from the title, which is the opposite of all my other books. I struggle with titles after I've written the book. Not this one. Librarians are a bit of a mystery to me; their job is more multifaceted than I realized. I had to do some research and read stories from real librarians. I wanted to stay away from the stereotype, though perhaps Sean fits it some ways. I love the role reversal of the confident (though not always) female character, and the somewhat nerdy, super smart librarian.

If you enjoyed the book and would like an email of my next release, please sign up for my newsletter @elizabeth-castle.com/contact. Please be assured that your email will never be sold (I wouldn't want mine sold, so I wouldn't do that to someone else). You can also follow me on Facebook @ facebook.com/elizabethcastle.romanceauthor.

Also, if you enjoyed this book, or any of my other titles, please consider leaving a rating at your favorite retailer, Goodreads and/or Bookbub. And if you have the time, a text review would be lovely. Indie authors rely on readers like you to tell others how much you enjoy their books.

Happy reading,

Lizzy Castle

Books by Elizabeth Castle

Single Titles:

   Going Home
   This Kind Of Love
   Chasing Hope
   The Babe & The Librarian (novella)

The Heart's Way Series:
   For Now and Always
   Ask Me To
   Say You Love Me
   Forever Love

Bennett Family Series:
   This Time Love
   A Bride For David
(novella)

All Of Me Series:
   All Of My Days
   All Of My Nights

Cantwell Quartet:
   Falling Slowly
   Unraveled
   Hidden Away
   Entangled

Contemporary "retro" Romance Series:
   Loving Jordan

Visit elizabeth-castle.com for newsletter sign up and up-to-date releases.

## Chapter One

Matt Henney pulled up in front of the newly finished ranch house. He slammed the door of his pickup and breathed in the fresh spring air, taking in the woods and canyons in the distance. Behind the canyon, snow-capped mountains set the backdrop to what he would now call home. The snow was melting, and summer wasn't far away. Every tense muscle in his body loosened as peace settled in. Of all the places he'd been in the world, he felt most at peace in Utah. Mountains, canyons, deserts, heat, and snow could all be found within its borders.

He looked around the vast property. He finally had the stake he needed to buy into his friends' business. No more traveling. No more open roads. No more scraping together every penny.

His gaze wandered off into the distance toward the canyon, far past where the ranch house stood. The cabins, horse trails, barns, and stables were quiet. He could see horses and cattle grazing. The Waters Ranch was a combination working ranch and retreat that was open year-round to guests, but the start of the busy season was still a month away. Guests could enjoy the luxurious hotel or rent one of the many guest cabins with the canyons and mountains in the background. They could go climbing, hiking, camping, or horseback riding. From the working ranch side, there was a small herd of cattle, goats, and chickens. The vast fields and orchard grew a variety of fruits and vegetables. Matt was content doing whatever was needed, whether it was working at the barns or taking guests out.

He turned to the house as the screen door opened. Allie Waters came down the four stairs of the porch and launched herself at him. Her strong arms held him tight as he caught her up. "I can't believe you're finally here."

A tall, dark-haired man followed at a slower pace. "She was worried you might not make it before dark."

Matt hugged his other friend. He and Jeremy Waters had been friends since childhood. "I wanted to see the sunset.

Nothing like it on Earth.”

Allie hugged him again. “It’s so good to see you.”

Matt set a hand on Allie’s stomach. When she’d told him she was pregnant, he’d been thrilled for her. They’d been friends since they’d served as medics in the army. When Matt had brought Allie home for a visit while on leave, Jeremy had taken one look at her and had fallen in love. It had amused him to see his ladies’ man best friend become tongue-tied around the forceful Allie. Allie hadn’t been particularly interested in marriage, but time and patience had worn her down.

Matt followed his friends inside, thinking about how different they were, yet how they complemented each other. Jeremy was much taller than his five-foot-eleven frame and dwarfed his five-foot-five wife. Jeremy’s hair was almost black, whereas Allie’s was shades of brown and red. Allie was the spitfire; the one who would always tell you exactly what she was thinking. Jeremy was just as forceful but did it in a quiet way.

“I see you two have been busy. Last time I saw this place, it was still bare drywall.” Matt gazed around the now-completed space. The open space was painted in light desert colors but filled with lush plants. The oversized glass windows and skylights brought the outdoors in. The tile floors were a jarring turquoise but somehow fit the space.

Allie settled her palms across her full belly. "Who knew Jeremy was so good at interior design?"

Jeremy came up behind her, wrapped his arms around her, and his hands settled on top of hers. "One of us had to be. Matt, your new trailer arrived last week. We've got it all up and running for you."

Allie had wanted him to build a house on the property, but Matt had declined. It wasn't his land yet, and his money was better spent helping build up the ranch. But neither did he want to spend all of his time camping, nor take up space in one of the cabins. So, he'd compromised and let them hook up a trailer for him.

Allie leaned into her husband. "Your furniture arrived, what little there was of it. Jeremy ordered a few extra pieces, and I stocked the kitchen, though you're welcome to eat with us."

"How about a tour?" Matt was impressed by the space.

It was homey, something neither he nor Jeremy knew much about. They'd both been in the foster system and had grown up in the same home. And while he had fond memories of his foster parents, neither he nor Jeremy were what you'd call home bodies.

Allie showed him around their finished home. He envied his friends. They had found each other and had built a business from the ground up. Matt accepted the cup of coffee when they settled into the kitchen. "It's hard to believe what this place used to be."

Allie inhaled the coffee before handing her husband his. "We've hired more staff. And with you finally settling in and buying in, we'll have more groups going out. Rock climbing is big business out here. I'll feel much better keeping Jeremy closer to home and letting you take the groups out."

Jeremy finished his coffee. "No rest for the weary. Hope you're ready, Matt. Allie has a new stud arriving tomorrow. Travis is going to take a new group camping at the mesa. Mike is taking out a newbie group of rock climbers. The renovations on the older cabins are finished, and we're going to start listing them to rent."

Matt rose and stretched. "Wherever you need me."

"Mmm. First problem might be in your trailer finishing cleaning it up."

Allie glared at her husband over her shoulder. "Cut her some slack. She's trying."

Jeremy released her and went to rinse their cups. "That woman hasn't worked a day in her life."

Matt glanced at Allie's pinched lips. "Problem?"

Jeremy replied. "Hope Whitfield. The woman is useless. Allie refuses to let me fire her. She showed up here last month along with a dozen other women looking to get hired. She had no job experience at all. Allie felt sorry for her and gave her a job anyway."

That surprised Matt. Allie was a firm believer in hard work and earning your way. She had to be tough leading a team of medics in the army. "Going soft on me?"

Allie gave him a dirty look. "There has got to be something she's good at. She's a body, and she's willing to work."

Jeremy shook his head. "I booted her out of the kitchen.

She couldn't seem to manage taking reservations and answering phones. Now she's the slowest member of our cleaning staff. The woman can barely make a bed. The other housekeepers are complaining. I'm going to assign her to the barn. Because, Allie, if the woman can't rake out a stall, then she's gone."

Allie relented. "All right. You made your point. School is out soon, and we'll have some new applicants."

Matt yawned, the long trip catching up with him. "Why don't I go check out the trailer and settle in."

Jeremy set a hand on Allie's shoulder. "I'll take him. You need to put your feet up."

Allie lifted her mouth to his. "Yes, dear."

Jeremy kissed her. "Come on, Matt. Hopefully, she didn't burn the place down."

Matt followed Jeremy in his truck as his friend led him down the dirt and gravel road. It took a couple of minutes to drive to where the trailer was nestled near some large boulders. He grabbed his bag from the passenger seat. "This is a lot nicer than I told you to get."

Jeremy agreed. "It is. But Allie said there was no way she

was letting that eyesore of a trailer you picked out anywhere near her property."

The trailer was single-wide, but from the length of it, it likely had a couple of bedrooms.  A large window, along with smaller windows, ran the length of the trailer. A small deck held a table and chairs, as well as a grill, and there was a large fire pit nearby.

"Allie wanted to be sure you stuck around.  And she said to think of it as a retreat when you come back from taking a bunch of greenhorns camping or climbing."

Matt opened the door and took in the space.  There was a large kitchen to the right with plenty of cabinets, full-size appliances, and a small island.  To the left, there was a full living room, a massive television, an empty bookcase, a couch, and a wood-burning fireplace.  There was a short hall that led to three doors.

Jeremy let the screen door shut behind him.  He called out, "Ms. Whitlock."

A woman came from the back room, rubbing her palms on her khakis.  She was about Allie's height, with chin-length auburn curls around an oval face.  The pants were loose on her frame, the dark blue polo shirt tucked in. The clothes were baggy, but he could see hints of curves underneath. She was pretty enough, but he agreed with Jeremy. There wasn't much to her, and she didn't appear sturdy enough to tackle the jobs on a retreat or ranch this size. She didn't look like she could weed a vegetable garden.

Her voice was soft when she spoke. "I finished up. The bed is made up, and I washed the bathroom down. I made sure everything was stocked in the kitchen like Mrs. Waters asked."

The woman's turquoise eyes glanced at him. He could tell from the expression on her face that she was nervous.

Jeremy poked his head into the bathroom and bedroom. "All right. You can go. We'll talk tomorrow."

Turquoise eyes once again held his. It was disconcerting. The anxiety had faded, and there was nothing else in her gaze, not even relief that she could go. She quickly brushed past the two men and was out of sight by the time he went to the window. "Not much to her."

"No. Allie took a shine to her. No clue why. Allie swears she knows her. But she doesn't recall knowing a

Whitfield or a Hope. But I don't have time, and neither does the rest of the staff, to tolerate someone who can't pull their weight."

Matt tossed his duffle bag next to the couch. "Can't or won't?"

Jeremy scrubbed a hand over his face. "Can't. I can't put my finger on it, but there's something wrong with her. The only reason I haven't fired her yet is that she puts in the hours. She works hard. It's just that nothing seems to get done. I don't know. For Allie's sake, I hope she can handle a rake, feed bags, or something. I will have to let her go."

Matt dropped onto the sofa. "Why don't I show her the ropes tomorrow? It's been a while since I've worked with the horses. Worse case, she can clean up after the goats."

Jeremy just shook his head. "In addition to the goats, Allie got a pair of alpacas. She also got some sheep. At the rate we're going, we could open a petting zoo. I didn't mind the cows and goats. The small farm Allie runs over on the east part of the property makes her happy. Milk and cheese fetch decent prices. Costly though. The apple and cherry orchards had a good harvest last year, and we're hoping for a repeat. Despite the small oasis we have here, we've got the desert to the south and canyons and mountains surrounding us. We're blessed this land has plenty of water to sustain our operations. Honestly, though, the sheep and alpacas are a bit much, even if they earn their keep. Can't say the same about Hope Whitfield."

Matt saw Jeremy off and checked out the rest of the trailer. The large king bed was met with approval and appreciation. The bathroom was spacious. It had a soaking tub and shower combo. The double vanity was more than he needed but was nice. There was a second empty bedroom tucked between the utility room and the master, though it would only hold a twin bed and a small dresser. Maybe he would tuck a desk in there. He didn't own much and didn't need much room. This place was a palace in comparison to some of the places he'd lived. But it afforded him privacy, a roof over his head, and a place to settle down.

It had taken him the last five years to finish saving up the stake he needed to buy into Allie and Jeremy's business. Allie had inherited the run-down retreat from her aunt on her mother's side of the family. They had wanted to bring him in years ago, but he wanted to be able to contribute to the operation, not just be an employee. They were his best friends, and they understood his need to own something of his own. He came during the busy summer season and spent the rest of the year in some of the coldest, harshest land out there, saving every penny. He'd survived, but this time he was staying for good.

* * *

Hope shivered as she poured the last of the jug of water over her head and rinsed out the shampoo. The temperature dropped at night, but it was just as cold in the mornings. At least this way her hair would be dry by the morning. When she'd first arrived and had to start taking camp baths, she'd cropped her longer hair to her chin. It was harder to control the shorter curls, but easier to wash and rinse.

She tossed a few more branches on the small fire as she blotted water out of her hair. She combed it out as close to the heat as she dared. She'd gotten good at camp baths and learned to use the least amount of water possible. Water was scarce on this side of the river. Her camp was surrounded by rocks and boulders, the lower level of the canyon surrounding the borders of the property. The river was a good mile or more from where she sat. Thankfully she was able to fill water jugs each night after work. If she was lucky, she could sneak some food out, as well. Tonight she had been cleaning the trailer, so she had missed dinner. Her stomach growled, but she ignored it.

She sat for a while with her flannel nightgown wrapped around her legs and let the fire warm her. The tarp she had staked into the ground kept the dirt and sand off her. Her work clothes were airing out on a nearby fence, and she idly thought it was time to make a trip into town. But not tonight. Millions of stars lit up above her as she felt her eyes start to droop. She yawned, knowing it was getting late, but too tired to grab her watch and look at the time.

Hope opened the flap to the tent she'd pitched near the run-down house. After her first night inside the house, she hadn't slept in it again. Spiders, bugs, rats, and who knew what else had made what was left of the house their home.

She hadn't intruded again.

"Ready for bed, Trixie?"

The massive dog raised her head. She didn't know a lot about dogs, but the vet who treated Trixie for a skin condition told her the dog was expensive. The vet's best guess was that she was likely a purebred Boerboel, a type of mastiff. Hope had been terrified the first time she'd laid eyes on Trixie. But the poor dog had been abandoned and left to starve. She had been so thin, her skin mottled, and her fur missing. Once fed and medicated, the dog slowly healed. She still had some scars, but the beautiful gold of her fur was now thick and healthy.

Hope doused the remainder of the fire and crawled inside the tent. The dog followed her inside, and Hope zipped them in. The dog lay down on the bed Hope had set up for her, and Hope climbed onto her air mattress. The dog immediately began snoring, but sleep eluded Hope. Her body was exhausted, but her mind wouldn't shut off.

"We'll talk tomorrow." That didn't bode well. Hope was surprised Jeremy Waters hadn't fired her yet. But Hope was desperate. She prayed he would give her another chance to prove she could be useful. Without the job at the Waters Ranch, she didn't know what she'd do. They were miles from a city. Miles from a town, even. Her car got her back and forth to work, and into town now and again, but it needed maintenance. She simply didn't have the money to put into it. The oil change last month was all she could afford.

She rolled onto her side, pulling the sleeping bag higher over her shoulders. By morning she'd be completely inside of it. Hope wasn't sure she was looking forward to the heat that would soon be heading her way, but it had to be better than the frigid temperatures she was currently experiencing.

She watched Trixie as she shifted to get more comfortable. Other than feeding Trixie and giving her affection, the dog took care of herself. When Hope came back from work each day, Trixie was still there. Hope didn't dare tie her up. There were wild animals, and tethering the dog could prove fatal.

Burrowing deeper, Hope closed her eyes. Matt Henney. Now he was a fresh drink of water. He was tall, likely around six feet, though he was a bit shorter than her employer. His hair was too long, longer than hers, and the gold, wavy locks went past his shoulders. The beard needed a trim but added to his rugged appearance. His biceps bulged at the edges of his t-shirt, and his chest and shoulders were broad. His eyes were a deep brown against his tanned skin. He was older than her; she'd put him close to forty. Fine wrinkles framed his eyes, but there was no gray hair at his temples, though a few sprinkled his beard and mustache. Dark wash jeans worn through the knees hugged muscular thighs.

She'd heard from one of the women who worked at the retreat tell some other women that he spent his summers here. He was a rock climber and survivalist. He took groups hunting, fishing, and camping, as well as taking advanced climbers to the nearby canyons. There was also a lot of feminine speculation about him. Rumors were that he was single. From some of the comments Hope had heard, even if he were in a relationship, that wouldn't stop some of the women from pursuing him. But gossip was that he was here to stay, and a couple of women were looking to be the first, or perhaps the next, Mrs. Henney.

He had a rugged appeal, and she wasn't immune now that she'd seen him for herself. She didn't know what possessed a person to pit themselves against nature, though these past two months living outside had given her a new appreciation for those who did. Give her a soft bed and a hot shower any day. And what she wouldn't give for hot running water. The hotel she stayed in from time to time had tepid water at best. But it had a coin-operated washer and dryer, the beds weren't full of bugs, and the price was right. And it rented by the hour, so she was able to get a room, have a nap, and wash her clothes before heading back to her "home."

It was hard to remember what home used to be. As a young girl, home was a two-story brownstone on the east coast. She'd seen pictures but didn't have real memories of it. As an adult, home was a garish mansion on the West Coast. She'd rather live outside for the rest of her life than ever set foot inside that marble entryway again.

Hope curled up tighter inside the sleeping bag as she shivered. She'd rather wear secondhand clothes than ever wear another designer suit. In a rage, she'd tossed out every article of clothing, every shoe. She'd had enough sense to sell the jewelry she owned. She still had a few pieces left to sell for emergencies. Likely the diamond bracelet would soon pay for her car. But only if Jeremy Waters didn't fire her in the morning. She'd need that bracelet to eat and to keep Trixie in kibble if he did.

*Want more? Get your copy of Chasing Hopet today.*